Nonna's Hanukkah Surprise

In loving memory of Nonna – K.F.

Text copyright © 2015 by Karen Fisman
Illustrations copyright © 2015 by Martha Avilés

KAR-BEN PUBLISHING
A division of Lerner Publishing Group, Inc.
241 First Avenue North
Minneapolis, MN 55401 USA
1-800-4-KARBEN

Website address: www.karben.com

Main body text set in 17/24 pt. Italia Std.
Typeface provided by Adobe Systems.

Library of Congress Cataloging-in-Publication Data

Fisman, Karen.
     Nonna's Hanukkah Surprise / by Karen Fisman ; illustrated by Martha Aviles.
       pages   pm
     Summary: When Rachel loses the special menorah her mother gave her so she could
share Hanukkah with her cousins, Rachel's grandmother comes to the rescue with a
creative and crafty solution.
     ISBN 978-1-4677-3476-9 (lib. bdg. : alk. paper)
     ISBN 978-1-4677-3477-6 (pbk. : alk. paper)
     ISBN 978-1-4677-8840-3 (EB pdf)
     [1. Hanukkah—Fiction. 2. Menorah—Fiction. 3. Lost and found possessions—Fiction.
4. Grandmothers—Fiction.] I. Avilés Junco, Martha, illustrator. II. Title.
PZ7.1.F57No 2015
     [E]—dc23   2014028813

Manufactured in the United States of America
1 – CG – 7/15/15

Nonna's Hanukkah Surprise

Karen Fisman

illustrated by Martha Avilés

KAR-BEN
PUBLISHING

"Do we have to go?" asked Rachel, trying to keep her voice from wobbling.

Mom looked surprised. "You love visiting Daddy's family," she said.

"But we'll miss Hanukkah!" said Rachel. "Nonna and the cousins celebrate Christmas."

"Don't worry, honey," said Daddy. "The rest of my family does celebrate Christmas. But we'll bring Hanukkah along, too. You'll see— it will be fun for us to share our holiday celebrations."

"Look," said Mom. She opened a small suitcase. It was filled with Hanukkah decorations, dreidels, chocolate Hanukkah gelt, and enough candles for all eight nights of Hanukkah. There was also a pile of gifts on the bed—both for Rachel and for her cousins.

Rachel felt a bit better. But something was missing.

"There's no Hanukkah menorah," she pointed out. "How will we light the Hanukkah candles?"

"Here, Rach," Daddy said, handing her a box. "An early Hanukkah present for you. Open it."

Inside was the best menorah Rachel had ever seen. Each of its branches was shaped like a person—and not just any person. This menorah had nine proud Maccabees, each holding a candle, including one for the shammash.

Rachel loved the story of the Maccabees, the brave Jewish fighters who defeated King Antiochus. She did think it was unfair, though, that the Maccabees were all boys. Rachel was sure that if she'd lived in the days of Antiochus, she would have been a Maccabee, too.

That was why this particular menorah was the very best.
All nine Maccabees were girls!

Rachel gave Daddy a big hug. "OK," she said with a smile. "We'll bring Hanukkah with us to Nonna and the cousins."

A week later, Rachel's family took a taxi to the airport. Mom was in charge of the Hanukkah suitcase, but Rachel was in charge of the Maccabee menorah, which was safe in her very own backpack.

On the plane, Rachel carefully tucked the menorah under the seat in front of her. Then she buckled her seat belt and waited for takeoff.

The next thing Rachel knew, Daddy was shaking her shoulder.
"Wake up, Rach. We're landing!"

Everyone stood up and shuffled into the aisle. Mom was already opening the overhead bin to take out the Hanukkah suitcase. Sleepy Rachel lurched to her feet and followed her family to the exit.

In the airport, Nonna and the cousins were waiting. There were lots of hugs and even more kisses. Nonna gave Rachel the biggest hug of all. Rachel took a deep breath, smelling Nonna's perfume—Nonna always wore lots, so everyone could enjoy it. She even saved her perfume bottles, because, she said, they were too beautiful to throw away.

"I'm so glad you're here, *bella,*" said Nonna in her heavy accent.

"Me too, Nonna," said Rachel, and she meant it.

As soon as Rachel stepped inside Nonna's house, she caught the scent of evergreens and a whiff of Nonna's famous *panettone*. Nonna took Rachel straight to the kitchen and cut her a thick slice of the sweet, fruit-filled bread.

"I'm making all my special foods for Christmas," Nonna said proudly. Then she winked. "And we're going to have Hanukkah, too. Don't you worry. You brought everything we need, yes?"

Rachel nodded. "Mom has decorations and lots of other stuff. And I..."

She stopped. She had been about to say "I have the menorah." But she didn't have the menorah! It was still on the plane. How could she have forgotten it?

A giant lump grew in Rachel's throat.

"What's wrong, *bella?*" asked Nonna.

Rachel ran to her parents. "I left the Maccabee menorah on the plane," she cried.

"Oh, sweetie," said Mom. "It's OK. We'll call the airport in the morning."

"But tonight is the first night of Hanukkah," sobbed Rachel. "We have to light the candles."

"We'll still light candles," said Daddy. "We just won't get to use your Maccabee menorah tonight. But we'll put up the decorations, play dreidel, and eat latkes like we always do. Don't worry, honey. It will be OK."

Mom opened her suitcase. The cousins swarmed around, reaching for decorations and spinning the dreidels on the kitchen table. But not Rachel. Her beautiful menorah was stuck on the plane, and it was all her fault.

Rachel rested her head on the kitchen table. She wished she could just go back home.

Then she smelled perfume and heard a whisper in her ear. "Teach me about the menorah, *bella*," said Nonna. "Then I'm going to make you feel better."

In a quiet voice, without even lifting her head, Rachel explained about the menorah. She told Nonna how it had eight candle holders for the eight nights of Hanukkah, and one extra for the shammash, the worker candle that lights the rest. And how, on the first night of Hanukkah, Jews light one candle plus the shammash, with another candle added each night, until on the last night all eight are lit.

"OK," said Nonna. "Now I know, so now I'll fix. But first I need my super-duper glue."

Nonna took the glue from a drawer. Then she slipped two Hanukkah candles out of Mom's suitcase and marched out of the room.

A few minutes later, Nonna was back—holding a beautiful, sparkling menorah! Nine glimmering crystal perfume bottles stood on a silver tray—all stuck in place with Nonna's super-duper glue!

The tallest bottle held the shammash, and another held the first candle of Hanukkah.

A smile spread over Rachel's face. It wasn't her girl Maccabee menorah, but it was a very special menorah all the same.

Rachel ran over and gave Nonna an enormous hug.

"Thank you, thank you, Nonna," said Rachel, not letting go.

When it got dark, everyone gathered around the glittering menorah.
Mom sang the blessing and Dad lit the first Hanukkah candle.

Afterward, as Rachel munched on Nonna's lasagna and Mom's potato latkes, she decided that bringing Hanukkah to Nonna and the cousins was pretty special. Maybe next time, she'd bring Purim!

About Hanukkah

On Hanukkah, an eight-day Festival of Lights, the Jewish people celebrate the victory of the Maccabees over the mighty armies of the Syrian king Antiochus. When they restored the Holy Temple in Jerusalem, the Maccabees found one jug of pure oil, enough to keep the Temple menorah burning for just one day. But, according to the story, a miracle happened and the oil burned for eight days. So on each night of the holiday an additional candle is added to the Hanukkah menorah (also called a hanukkiyah), which is lit with the shammash, the helper candle. It is traditional to exchange gifts, eat foods fried in oil—*latkes* (potato pancakes) and *sufganiyot* (donuts)—and play the dreidel game. A dreidel is a spinning top. The letters on its four sides are *nun, gimmel, hey,* and *shin,* which stand for "A Great Miracle Happened There." Hanukkah celebrates a time when the few defeated the many and religious freedom was restored.

About the author

Once upon a time, Karen Fisman worked as an equities analyst and did lots of writing for grown-ups. But when her kids were born, she discovered it was much more fun to write for children, and that's what she's been doing ever since. Karen lives in Toronto with her husband, her two kids and a schnoodle named Cocoa. Her previous children's books include *An Adventure in Latkaland* and *Problems in Purimville.*

About the illustrator

Martha Avilés was born and raised in Mexico City, where she still lives. She has illustrated many children's books including *Say Hello, Lily; The Shabbat Princess;* and the award-winning *Stones for Grandpa,* a Bank Street College Best Children's Book of the Year, Booklist Top 10 Religion and Spirituality Book for Youth, and Sydney Taylor Honor Award winner.